AF284498

Trapped

Love Wild

Bibliografische Information der Deutschen Nationalbibliothek:

Die Deutsche Nationalbibliothek verzeichnet diese Publikation in der Deutschen Nationalbibliografie; detaillierte bibliografische Daten sind im Internet über http://dnb.dnb.de abrufbar.

Herstellung und Verlag:
BoD – Books on Demand, Norderstedt

ISBN: 978-3-7534-9611-5

They say nobody knows what happens behind closed doors, and that there's always more than meets the eye. Even the most perfect of households have skeletons in their closets, and every now and again, one of them falls out. Take the Matthews family. They were a thirty-something couple without kids, your typical DINK family. Ian worked at a Honda dealership while Evelyn was a bank manager. They attended church every Sunday, ate out Friday nights, and according to everyone that knew them, their lives were the epitome of married life. However, not everything was as perfect as it seemed. As vibrant and attractive as they both were, one very important part of their marriage was seriously lacking: the bedroom.

While Evelyn tried everything possible under the sun to entice and seduce her husband, Ian was simply uninterested. The rare times that he was able to muster up the will to try to make love to his wife, he always fell short, leaving Evelyn frustrated and horny. Left to her own devices, she took to masturbating whenever she felt the urge, but she saw this as a quick fix to a growing issue. She was timid by nature, and never into any kind of kinks or sex toys, so her options were limited, to say the least. Hands can only do so much, and every now and again she craved something more. Too embarrassed to talk to anybody about their problems, they both went on with their jobs and their lives as if nothing in the world was wrong, but just below the surface, the pot was beginning to boil over.

Like most couples, everything had been wonderful in the beginning: flowers, dates, and the sex was at least passable. Over the years, everything wound down to a relatively comfortable routine. But Evelyn wanted more. Even though she knew in the back of her mind that Ian was definitely the ideal husband, she dreamed of having a loving, passionate man to give her rough, passionate sex. One night, a week before their anniversary, she decided to take matters into her own hands and seduce her husband. After making a light dinner of chicken breasts over rice pilaf, she put on an old babydoll that she hadn't worn in years, hoping to bring back some good memories. Humming softly to herself, she pulled her hair up into a messy bun, brushing on some lip gloss as she sat at the kitchen table and waited. Hearing Ian's car pulling into the driveway, she jumped to her feet and lit a cigarette, a vice that she indulged in on occasion. Hearing the front door open, she blew a perfect smoke ring just as he walked into the kitchen, following the smell of the food.

"Smells wonderful, honey. What in the world are you doing?" he asked in consternation, frowning at the lit cigarette in her hand that was threatening to ash onto the tile floor. "Since when do you smoke in the house? And right next to the food?" his face turned beet red, as did Evelyn's.

"I wanted to surprise you..." she trailed off, putting out the cigarette and doing a model turn in front of him. "We've both had a rough week, so I figured why not take the edge off?" she asked suggestively. At this, Ian seemed to calm down and rethink his words.

Coming towards her, he wrapped his arms around her and kissed her gently on the lips, making her smile.

"That's my baby," she purred, pressing her slender body against his. But something was missing. While any normal man would jump at the chance to devour her, with her svelte figure, barely clad in lingerie,

Ian didn't get remotely hard. "Babe, do I not turn you on anymore?" she pulled away, looking him straight in the eye, not daring to breathe.

"Of course you do!" Sighing sharply, Ian shook his head. "Let's just eat, hm? I'm telling you, it smells like you outdid yourself tonight." Sitting down, he helped himself to a plate while Evelyn rushed back into the bedroom to put on something much more sensible for a quiet, boring dinner. Fighting back tears, she lent an ear to Ian's work stories, amazed at the fact that he had the ability to forget his wife half naked in the kitchen in record time.

That Sunday, after the initial embarrassment had worn off and was more or less forgotten, the happy couple went to church. Barely paying attention to that week's service, Evelyn allowed her mind to wander while the pastor spoke about forgiveness and repentance. Sneaking a glance at her husband, she saw his face serious and concentrated, hanging on every word that was spoken. Chuckling to herself, she crossed her legs, fanning herself in the slightly stuffy church. Afterwards, they hung around to talk to a few acquaintances, when she saw Pastor George coming outside.

"Hold on a second," she excused herself, kissing Ian on the cheek as she hurried over to the one person that she was desperate enough to ask for help. "Pastor George!" she called out, catching up to him before he went into the church garden.

"Sister Evelyn!" he greeted, holding his hand out to shake hers vigorously. "So glad to see you. Did you enjoy service this morning?" Trying to control the blush that threatened to creep up her cheeks, she nodded, feeling horrible for lying to a clergyman.

"Always," she smiled. "But, um, I had a more personal matter that I... didn't know who to ask for help. Do you have a moment?"

"Of course I do. Come walk with me," he wrapped a comforting arm around her. "What seems to be the problem?"

"My husband and I... I feel like we're drifting apart. Things aren't like they used to be, and the worst part is, our anniversary is in a few days. I don't think he'll remember it, regardless. As much as I hate to use the phrase, there's just no spark. What do I do?"

"My first question has to be, have you gone to Brother Ian about this? He's the one you need to be talking to, Sister."

"I've tried... but he's just so stuck in his ways that he pretends that it's nothing! I'm at my wit's end, Pastor George. Maybe you have some spiritual guidance for me?"

she chuckled mirthlessly. He squeezed her shoulder reassuringly.

"Sister, forgive me, I have to be so blunt about this but… are you fulfilling him in your wifely duties? I preach the Holy Word, and teach others about fulfilment of the eternal soul, but I do understand, also, that we are all only human. I'm not ashamed to say that we all have needs. And intimacy *is* important in a marriage, as I'm sure the two of you are well aware."

"Yes, we are aware. Or, at least, I am. He's just not interested anymore. To be totally honest, Pastor, he was never all that interested to begin with; this issue didn't pop up overnight. I suppose I let it slide and I've been ignoring it all these years."

"I'm not entirely sure that I'm the correct person for this, but if you like, I'll talk to him one on one. Maybe I can get through to him?" he suggested kindly.

"Yes. *Please*. But don't let him know that I came to you first; he'll just clam up and it'll be useless at that point.

"You have my word. The last thing I want is to see yet another broken marriage. Go with God."

Feeling lighter, she pranced back to Ian and rubbed his shoulder affectionately. As they drove home, her phone chirped with a text. *I guess you're home from church right about now, so why don't you come by for some more communion wine? LOL.* Laughing, she saw that it was from her longtime friend Ruby, a single woman a few years younger than Ian and Evelyn. Evelyn secretly lived vicariously through her friend, especially since her sex life had taken such a nosedive; Ruby lived to meet, date, and fuck any man that caught her fancy, and she made no apologies. To her, sex was an activity that you did, primarily, for fun, and as an afterthought, for the purpose of procreation. Needless to say, she was not frequently seen in, or anywhere near, a church.

"Babe, Ruby wanted me to go over there for a bit. Did you want anything special for dinner or are you okay with some steaks and a loaded baked potato?"

"Uh, go ahead, Eve. Tell her I said hey when you see her."

Two hours and a bottle of Merlot later, both women were sitting and laughing in Ruby's living room.

"Man," Evelyn started, sipping from her long stemmed glass. "It's been a while, huh?"

"I try to tell you! But you're always busy being the perfect Stepford wife. *Not* that I'm knocking that either, because Ian is great," she added hastily. "You found your-self a good catch, my friend. Believe you me, that's not too common these days. I should know, I've test drove them all."

"I know it, I know it. But sometimes my good catch isn't the greatest in the world," she said glumly, staring into the murky contents of her glass. "But whatever, we're going to talk to Pastor George and it'll be fine. Or, rather, *I* spoke to him and he'll talk to Ian on my behalf."

"Uh oh. Trouble in paradise?" Ruby probed. "What, can he not get it up any-more? You guys are a little young to be deal-ing with that, aren't you?"

"Tell that to his dick," Evelyn blurted, hiccupping slightly. "Oops." Ruby's mouth hung open unattractively for a long moment before she caught herself and cleared her throat. "It's not like *that*, we're just going through a dry spell. It happens," she explained evasively.

"Then try something different. Maybe some outfits, toys, paddles," she rattled off. "Fun stuff. Make him wear your panties or something, then use a dildo on him!" Now it was Evelyn's turn to have her jaw drop.

"We're not into that stuff, Ruby!" she chastised. "Jeez, what kind of freak are you? We're a regular married couple."

"The kind that has satisfying sex whenever I want and with *whoever* I want," she replied unabashedly. "Don't look at me like that! You can talk to as many so called experts as you want to, but ultimately it's on the two of you. A relationship is built from the inside out, not the outside in, sweetie.

Even I know that, and I *hate* relationships with a passion." Feeling out of sorts Evelyn quickly changed the subject, and poured herself another glass, downing it in record time.

As predicted, the Matthews' anniversary came and went unnoticed. Try as she might, with a full course dinner and another attempt at seduction, nothing helped. That night, she placed his hands on her breasts, encouraging him to fondle her, and he actually did manage to penetrate her for a few minutes. Wrapping her legs around him, she bucked her hips wildly, wanting to take advantage of every second that she could.

"Fuck me, Ian, harder!" she panted, holding him close.

"I'm trying…" he whined. *No, no, no,* she silently chanted, well aware of what was to come next. Even as he tried to pump her, his cock softened until it slipped out of her cunt. Disappointed, she wiggled out from under him and turned over, too upset to try to soothe his ego.

Over the course of the next few weeks, she continued to mull over her friend's words, and thought that maybe Ruby had the right idea. As a bank manager, her job was relatively easy as long as there were no emergencies. Any other time, she stayed in her office and monitored the bank from there, watching the cameras and counting the tellers' drawers whenever they were pulled. Sitting at her computer, she grew restless as she randomly browsed the internet. On a whim, she searched 'sexy ideas for couples,' but found cheesy magazine articles, which were pretty much useless.

Biting her lip, she randomly looked up 'hardcore porn,' and found a whole wide world of new and previously unknown activities. Wide eyed, she scrolled through videos of men and women in some of the most unimaginable poses... and she found that it turned her on immensely. Checking to make sure that her door was locked, she threw a leg up on her desk, making her knee length pencil skirt hike up. Pushing her panties aside, she spread her swollen lips and plunged two fingers deep into her throbbing cunt. Holding back a moan so that nobody would hear her, she sucked in her bottom lip and exhaled harshly, the wet squelching sound of her pussy exciting her even more as she watched a video of two men filling up a petite brunette, rotating through all three holes in turn. She wondered fleetingly how that would feel, as the brunette wore an expression of ecstasy while she held her ass cheeks open for one man while simultaneously deep throating the second one. As she came, her body jerked violently, and she nearly bit through her lip in an attempt to hold back her cries of pleasure.

Breathless, she couldn't move for a minute while trying to collect herself. Her office phone ringing made her jump so badly that she nearly toppled over; scrambling for it, she hastily adjusted her clothes with her free hand.

"Evelyn Matthews," she answered in a harried voice. "How can I help you today?"

"Well hello, Mrs. Matthews," Ruby's cheerful voice boomed over the line. "You can help me by joining me for lunch, since I'm in the area right now. What time works for you?" Laughing, she sat up and brushed a stray strand of hair out of her eyes.

"It's not too busy today, so I can leave right now, if you want. Where exactly are you?"

"Uh, try waiting in line for a teller so I can make a deposit before I grab a bite," she giggled.

"Okay, I'm coming out now."

Walking arm in arm down the sunny street, Ruby regaled Evelyn with yet another one of her various wild stories.

"So he bent me over my balcony and you know how chilly it was last night! God, I was freezing my tits off, literally!" she was saying to a laughing Evelyn.

"But I bet *he* kept you warm," she nudged her friend. "Or was *that* cold too?"

"Oh, not at all, honey. Yeah, that warmed me right up. It wasn't as big as I'm used to but for him, I'll make an exception…I'm thinking of seeing him to-night, too."

"Ruby…I watched porn at work to-day," Evelyn blurted, unable to hold back any longer. Staring at her blankly, Ruby waited for her to finish speaking.

"And?" she prompted as they reached the diner. "People do that all the time. What's the big deal?" They sat down and ordered two coffees, poring over the menu until the waitress was out of earshot.

"I *liked* it," Evelyn admitted in a low voice. "I guess it's just been a while, that's all. I forgot what good, raunchy sex is!"

"Oh, well if that's the only issue, you should have told me. Come over and watch Loverboy tonight, we have a few tricks up our sleeves." Laughing at Evelyn's stunned expression, she dabbed the corner of her mouth with a napkin. "I'm serious!" As they placed their orders, it gave Evelyn a chance to weigh her options. It was all well and good for her crazy, unattached friend to live freely and openly, but *she* was a married woman. A married woman who wasn't having sex with her husband. That thought alone was the deciding factor and as she dug into her chicken salad, she nodded.

"I'll be there."

That afternoon, she came home to Ian lying on the couch watching television on his off day.

"Hey, babe," he said absently when she walked into the living room on her way upstairs. Changing her mind, she tossed her purse aside and headed back for the couch. "Hey!" he said in surprise as Evelyn straddled him.

"Have you been sitting here all day?" she asked as she kissed his neck. "While I've been sitting behind a desk at work?"

"No, I did some yardwork earlier," he wrapped his arms around her tightly, holding her close. "Mmm…" Giggling, she slid her hand in between them and rubbed the rapidly forming bulge.

"After a long, hard day, all I want is something long and hard." Unzipping his jeans, she freed his erection and stroked it languidly. Lowering her head, she took his member into her mouth gently, at first, wanting to savor his taste. Sucking a little harder, she tasted the salty precum, making her want more. Maneuvering her hand without letting go of his cock, she massaged his balls, squeezing them and laughing inwardly at the groan that escaped from Ian's mouth.

"Okay, babe," he whispered after a few more minutes. "Why don't we finish this tonight?" he sat up, pulling away from Evelyn's hot mouth. Chancing a quick glance down, she noticed that his cock was swiftly softening.

"What?" she asked, astounded. "Why?"

"Because," he helped her to her feet. "I want to have plenty of time with you." It was all she could do to keep from rolling her eyes at this empty promise.

"Okay. Anyway, I'm heading out a few to go hang out with Ruby. I'll fix something for dinner before I leave, though."

"Sounds good." Ian headed towards the kitchen, and Evelyn heard the back door slam shut. *Unbelievable,* she thought as she stomped up the stairs angrily.

While she made a quick dinner, she fumed. Ian was on a business call in the den, and she was glad to not have him hovering over her. Taking the chicken out of the frying pan, it struck her that she couldn't wait to get over to Ruby's place. She thought of the porn that she had watched at work, and it turned her on all over again.

"Honey?" Ian's voice broke through her thoughts and she spun around.

"Yeah? Dinner's ready."

"Pastor George called and invited us for dinner. But didn't you say you had plans?" he asked. Blushing, Evelyn nodded.

"That's right. And that's a bit last minute… you already have dinner waiting for you here."

"Uh huh. Maybe I'll stop by for an after dinner cigar or something," he said nonchalantly. Picking up a piece of chicken, Evelyn shrugged.

"Sounds like a plan. Ian?" she cracked her knuckles, something she only did when she was edgy.

"What's up?" he smiled innocently at her, making her nearly lose her nerve. *Nah, forget it,* she reasoned with herself. *I shouldn't do this...*

"Are you still...attracted to me?" she held her breath, unsure of whether or not she was ready to hear "no."

"Why wouldn't I be?" he chortled. "You're my wife, you're gorgeous, and I have no complaints," he said patiently. "Where is all this coming from?"

"I mean, we barely have sex. And when we do... it's like you're not into it."

"You sound stressed," he countered. "Go, go have fun with Ruby. Get your mind off of whatever it is that's bothering you, and tell her I said hi. Okay?"

By the time she finally made it to Ruby's apartment, she was not alone. Answering the door in a skimpy bathrobe and a belt in her hand, Evelyn was not sure what she was in for.

"Hiya!" Ruby opened the door wider to let her in. "What held you up? We had to get started without you, girl."

"Um, Pastor George invited us to dinner, but I passed. I think Ian went alone though, just to not be rude and turn him down."

"Uh huh," Ruby smiled knowingly. "You had that old fart talk to your husband, didn't you? I told you that your issues should be between the two of you! Not some Jesus freak with a stick up his ass."

"So!" she changed the subject. "Where's your little friend?" Entering Ruby's bedroom, she found a tall, lean muscled man kneeling at the foot of the bed. "Oh."

"Hi," he said shyly.

"Did I *say* that you could speak, dog?" Ruby cut in harshly. "What did I tell you?"

"Speak only when spoken to," he lowered his gaze to the ground, as Evelyn looked on in amazement.

"That's right. And now you'll have to be punished." Grabbing an old college text-book off her small shelf, she tossed it at the man. "Here you go. Oh, Evelyn, this is Randy, by the way. But we'll refer to him as 'dog' to-night. He knows his place."

With her heart pounding in anticipation, she stepped back and watched Ruby use her bare foot to shove Randy down onto his back. For a split second, she really could see him as a dog, and she had to hold back her laughter.

"Be a good pup and lick momma's feet," she cooed, wiggling her toes above his head. To Evelyn's shock, he stuck his tongue out and tried to reach her foot, but she pulled it away at the last moment. "Ah, ah, ah! Good boys ask for it, don't they?"

"Please!" he begged. "Please, give it to me, mommy." Giggling, she shoved her big toe into his mouth and the look on his face as he sucked it was one of pure pleasure.

"Wow." The word slipped out of her mouth before she could catch herself and remember that she was supposed to be an observer. "You suck her toe like you're sucking a cock." There was absolute silence for a moment, while Randy looked at Evelyn out of the corner of his eye, Ruby's toe still in his mouth.

"Who the hell told you to stop?" she barked. "Here, suck them all, since you're being a nosy bastard." With a little effort, she crammed the other four toes into his mouth, and he looked almost comical. Turning back to her friend, Ruby grinned. "He does, doesn't he?! And you're right, he is a good little cock sucker, too. I have the pictures to prove it. You just love momma's strap on, don't you?" she cooed to him. "Lick the bottoms of my feet, dog!" Wrenching her toes away from him, she all but stepped on his face while he dragged his tongue across her sole.

After a while of switching back and forth between her right and left foot, Ruby got bored. Yawning, she beckoned for Randy to sit up and, to her amazement, beckoned for Evelyn to come closer.

"Me? What do you need me for? I'm just here to watch."

"Yeah, but I need an extra set of hands," she urged. "Relax, it'll be easy." Going to her dresser drawer, she pulled out a plain box and set it on her king sized bed. Rooting through it, she pulled out her strap on. "I think this is pretty self-explanatory." Staring at it, Evelyn was at a loss for words.

"And I'm going to use it on the dog?"

"That's right! Bend over, dog. You know what to do." Scrambling to his feet, he assumed the position, his ass facing Evelyn. "Go ahead, hon, put it on."

Stepping into it gingerly, Evelyn felt way out of her league, but she would be lying to herself if she said she wasn't a little bit anxious to try it. Ruby whistled when she saw it, laughing appreciatively.

"That turns me on more than this little bitch here," she nudged Randy with her foot. "Come here and convince me to keep your mongrel ass around." Lying back and spreading her legs, Randy uses the tip of his tongue to part her lips and delve into her wet folds, making her squeal. Evelyn watched in aroused fascination as he traced tiny circles around her clit, and she subsequently forgot about the strap on until Ruby's voice broke her concentration. "Hey, someone needs to be getting fucked. His asshole is waiting for you."

"Oh!" grabbing his hips awkwardly, she tried to slide into him but was met with a little resistance. Spreading his cheeks, she used the tip to ease her way into his ass, and apparently she was doing the right thing because he pressed back against her in response. Encouraged by this, she slid the dildo all the way into him, and was pleased at his deep growl. *Shit, I didn't even use any lube*, she realized, but at this point it was too late, and Randy didn't seem to mind. He grabbed Ruby's legs harder, and Evelyn watched as her friend's hips bucked slightly.

"Fuck, you dirty dog. Lick this pussy, come on!" she yelped. Evelyn fucked Randy harder, feeling small beads of sweat begin to trickle from her temples. "Shit!" Ruby cried out as she came, grabbing the back of Randy's head. "Fuck! Make me cum again!"

Wanting to try something different, Evelyn pulled out of his ass and began spanking his ass with the dildo. His pale skin reddened quickly, and a lightbulb went off in her mind.

"Turn around, dog," she ordered him. "I have something for you." Ruby sat up interestedly, wondering if her mousy friend had, at long last, come out of her shell.

"You heard her." Obediently, he turned around and sat on the bed, his cock sticking straight up. *She was right, it isn't all that big but it's at least thick,* she thought approvingly. Evelyn swiped one finger across the tip, wiping off some of the precum that had beaded at the tip.

"You like that, *dog?* Ruby, get me ruler, will you?" Without bothering to fix her lingerie, she hopped off the bed and rushed around to get two rulers for her friend. Tossing one ruler aside, Evelyn tapped the other against her leg ominously. "Did you like getting fucked? Is that asshole nice and loose now?" He nodded mutely and she smacked his dick soundly with the wooden ruler.

Hearing him yelp, she grinned. His cock bounced amusingly and she smacked it down again for fun.

"Do you think I should let you cum?" she asked sweetly. "Think faster!" she slapped his balls and he grimaced in pain, yet his erection didn't go down. "You take way too long to answer questions, dog. Why don't I get your mommy to fuck you some more? If you're good, she might let you cum today. Then again, I can't speak for her." Hearing this, Ruby grabbed the other ruler and forced Randy off the bed and to his knees. As she spanked him mercilessly, Evelyn took the initiative to look for another dildo, even though she was still wearing the strap on. Grabbing a slightly smaller toy, she slid it easily into his ass and let go, leaving it stuck inside him. Laughing until tears began to pool in her eyes, she grabbed Ruby's arm.

"Look!" The two women burst into laughter, Ruby doubling over and holding her stomach.

"Walk around and bark, dog. Don't you *dare* make a mess on my carpet, either!" she commanded, tittering. To Evelyn's incredulity, he crawled around, barking randomly with the dildo still sticking out of his ass and bouncing with his every movement. "Just because you made me laugh today, I'll let you cum. But give us a minute, pup." He crawled out of the room, leaving them alone. "So?"

"Fucking awesome," Evelyn gushed. "I've never…"

"I can tell. But Randy can't."

"So… do I leave you to your private time or…?"

"Sure. I mean, if you want. You know I don't mind, you're always welcome," Ruby winked.

"Nah, I think I'll head home. You have fun."

Late that night, long after Ian was snoring like a chainsaw, Evelyn lay awake, still reeling from her earlier adventure. Even through her tiny twinge of guilt, she played every moment over and over in her mind as she turned onto her side. Luckily, the next day was Sunday and their day would be pretty much routine. As she fell into a deep sleep, she made a mental note to talk to Pastor George again, as her curiosity about the random dinner invitation was killing her.

Ian was, as usual, his normal attentive self, but something just seemed… *off*. It was something that Evelyn couldn't put her finger on, but there it was.

"And let us not forget the fallen cities of Sodom and Gomorrah, and how their downfall came to be," Pastor George intoned as other members nodded and clapped. "Instead, we should all strive to learn from Job. Even on our darkest day, we need to be able to say 'thank you, Jesus!'" A few other members shouted "thank you!" and one older woman stood up and clapped enthusiastically. Quelling the urge to roll her eyes, she peeked at her husband again, who sat still as stone in his seat, his eyes glassy. On impulse, she slipped her hand into his, and he squeezed back lightly.

Once service was over and they had both taken communion, Evelyn turned to tell Ian that she was going to say hello to Pastor George, but he caught her off guard and beat her to the punch.

"Pastor George was going to lend me a few books, you know, for some light reading on my down time. Um, want to wait for me in the car?" Raising an eyebrow, she felt cornered. *Damned if I do, and damned if I don't*, she thought. *Hopefully whatever advice he's giving Ian will help.*

"Sure, babe," she said aloud, pasting on a cheerful grin. "Tell him I said hello and that I'll be taking him up on that offer for dinner probably in the next week or so."

"Will do. I won't take long, you go ahead," he urged her, kissing her quickly through her hair. Sauntering outside into the cloudy day, she waved hi and made small talk with a few other church members, trying to pass some time while waiting for Ian. Little by little, however, people drove off until theirs was one of three cars still in the parking lot. Checking her watch, she saw that Ian had been away for over an hour and a half, and she began to worry. *Shit, I hope he's not telling Ian about what I said… dammit,* she reprimanded herself for opening up to someone so close to home about such a personal matter. *This looks like a job for… damage control,* she thought as she grabbed her purse and got out of the car.

Locking the car behind her, she stormed across the lot and back into the church, heading for Pastor George's office. Any other day, she would have had a little more respect and not made so much noise, but this time, she stomped her way up the steps and down the long marble hall to the small office. Without hesitation, she heaved the door open without knocking and nearly fainted from the shock. There they were, both naked and dripping with sweat, their bodies entwined clumsily in the office full of holy scripture. She didn't know which was worse: the sight of a revered church man naked with his cock wet and shining, whether

43

from spit or other bodily fluids was anybody's guess, or the sight of her husband with a man of the cloth.

"You have got to be shitting me right now," she tried to scream, but it came out a hoarse whisper. "This *can't* be happening."

"Baby…" Ian started, the guilt written all over his shining face. "I – I can explain – "

"Explain *what*?!" she let out a shout of crazed laughter. "That my husband and the pastor of my church are a pair of faggots? Save it!"

"Sister Evelyn, please!" Pastor George tried to calm her down, or at least get her to lower her voice. "Please, this is the house of God. We can't have this in here," he said in perfect hypocrisy.

And that's when she snapped. She stood stock still, her mind racing with so many wild thoughts that she could hardly keep up. Without uttering another word, she slammed the door shut and locked it behind her.

"You're right. This is the house of God, and I want Him to see how low down the two of you are. Ian, why don't you show me just how the kind Pastor likes to get his salad tossed? I bet it's a pretty hot scene, huh?" She was met with more silence, which only served to fuel her fire. "Are the two of you deaf? Ian, either you bend the good pastor over, or it'll be you getting a tongue in his ass. But you'd like that shit, you fucking pervert." Neither one could look her in the eye, so she knew it had to be true. "Yeah, I know I'm right."

"Baby, don't... we can explain."

"I could give a shit about your explanation," she snapped. "I really want to hear it from Pastor George's mouth."

Staring at him, she waited expectantly as the poor man struggled to find the right words to say.

"We didn't mean for this to happen," he started. "You must believe that, Sister!"

"Then how long have you two known that you were fags? Did this happen... because I asked you to talk to him?" she shot at the pastor. "Did you seduce my husband?" Fighting back tears, she then shot daggers at Ian. "Or were you always a closet case and this was just a valid excuse?"

"I've known for a while," Ian offered. "Years, honestly. That's why things had gone downhill for us. Well, in actuality, that's why things were never quite right. I told Pastor George some time ago about... how I felt. And things just happened from there. Again, please, I'm so sorry."

"You dirty motherfucker. You knew about this long before I came to you and you *consoled* me! You gave us communion every week!" she screamed. "What, you were putting wafer in his mouth at service, then replacing it with your cock afterwards? You sick freak! You know what? I think you should be the one to be bent over. Now!" Exchanging glances, they had no other choice; it was either do as she said, or have both their lives and reputations ruined, and they were not ready to face the music.

Inching forward, they were nearly nose to nose when Ian knelt in front of the pastor and stroked him back to life. The veins in his cock stuck out, and Pastor George could swear he even saw them pulsating as he looked down. Ian definitely felt it throbbing as he tried to make sense of what was happening. The sensation of having his foreskin pulled back once more was titillating as Ian took the tip of his tongue and gently tapped it against the tiny hole at the head, now freely dripping precum.

"Ahhh... fuck..." he groaned, clenching his eyes shut. He exhaled deeply and was about to open his eyes once more when he felt a warm sensation envelop his member. "*Jesus*," he cried. Ian bobbed his head up and down rapidly, holding onto the pastor's hips to gain leverage.

He sneakily let one hand creep up Pastor George's leg to his balls, grazing one with the tip of his nail. Stroking it gently with his index finger, he gently rubbed the little stretch of skin between his balls and his anus, knowing how much this turned him on, feeling his cock twitch wildly in his mouth. Taking this as a sign of encouragement, he lifted Pastor George's cock to tease the tight, puckered hole. Just as he was about to dip his finger into it, his concentration was broken.

"I think he's ready for you, *dear*," Evelyn insisted nastily. "I want to see some action." Obeying her, Ian turned the pastor around and held his ass cheeks apart, reminding Evelyn vividly of her adventure with Randy, only with the real thing instead of a strap on. He looked down admiringly at the pastor's body, then let his cock press against the flaming hot flesh, taking his time with his clandestine lover. Sensing their hesitation, her anger burst through and she snatched a bible off the desk, using it as a paddle to whip Pastor George's cock repeatedly. He howled in pain as she struck him, but pleasure overrode the sting of her blows when Ian shoved his cock as deep as he could into his lover.

Before her eyes, she watched her husband thrust into their admired pastor in one crude motion, the sound of skin slapping against skin echoing off the walls, though this might have been her imagination. For the first time, she saw how much Ian truly enjoyed sex… it just so happened to be with another man, not with her. By his jerking movements, Evelyn assumed that he was close to orgasm, and when he exploded a few short minutes later, his long, low groan was one of a hell of a finale. When Pastor George stood up, she even saw a minute trickle of cum drip from his hole.

"Bravo, both of you. Oh, and Pastor George, in case my husband didn't get a chance to tell you, I think I will take you up on your dinner offer sometime soon. But we must be going now; I still haven't gotten Sunday dinner on the *fucking* stove yet." Prodding Ian into getting dressed, they curtly exited the office, leaving a naked pastor standing by his desk in astonishment.

From then on, the Matthews household became a silent war zone, the tension thick, though there were no genuine arguments. The silence was more than enough to make both parties extremely uncomfortable in their own home. Too embarrassed to tell her best friend what was going on, Evelyn was distraught. On the other hand, Ian was walking on eggshells, well aware that there was no coming back from this one. He'd taken to sleeping in the den, even though his wife had not formally kicked him out of their bedroom. They both got around by avoiding the other, sneaking around their house like thieves to make sure they never met in the hallways, kitchen, etc.

Pretty soon, the pressure got to be too much for Evelyn, who called Ruby one day from work, unable to keep this to herself for one more second.

"Look who it is!" Ruby said snidely. "And here I thought you'd forgotten about little old me."

"Ruby, this is no time for jokes!" she hissed. "We need to talk ASAP!" Catching on, she put on her serious tone and Evelyn heard a rustle of papers on the other line.

"I can't do lunch today, but I can leave early. Does that work?"

"Yeah, yeah, sure. I'll come pick you up? It's urgent."

"Fine, see you then." It was then that it dawned on her that she had the rest of the day to stew in her own thoughts. At a complete loss, she paced her office, vaguely wishing that some type of emergency would crop up. Sitting back down, she checked her work emails and realized that she had to work on a promotional gimmick that had been set to launch a week ago. Luckily, it wasn't a huge thing, so it slipped through the cracks, though Evelyn did not want to chance it, either. Speeding through the paperwork and making a few calls to promotors was the perfect distraction to keep her occupied until the end of the day.

The two women met up at a diner close to Ruby's job, Evelyn pale and sallow skinned, and Ruby's face tense with worry.

"All right, missy. Are you going to tell me what's going on, or am I just here for moral support? Either one is fine but I'd rather know so that I can help you out." Evelyn was quiet for a long time, stirring her coffee rhythmically without realizing what she was doing. She didn't trust her voice, and she had to clear her throat a few times before speaking up.

"Something happened with Ian. And it was pretty bad," she began. Ruby opened her mouth to respond, but Evelyn stopped her before she lost her nerve. "Ian's been fucking Pastor George." For the first time that either woman could remember, Ruby was struck dumb; the usually witty tongue of hers had no response and no quip. "I caught them, naked, in his office after church... so I made Ian fuck him one more time. I don't know what came over me; all I could think of was the day I fucked Randy with your strap on and it just clicked in my head. And I kind of want to do it again. But I also want revenge. Fuck. What would *you* do?"

"Hold on. This is unbelievable. You mean to tell me that *your husband* is gay? All this time he's been gay?!" Ruby screeched, forgetting their surroundings. A few of the more nosy patrons at the corner diner turned around with quizzical looks.

"God dammit keep your voice down!" Evelyn whispered loudly, wanting to slap her crazy friend. "Look, there's no need to re-hash this because I've done it enough for both of us combined. What I *want* is to get them both back. Well, fuck Pastor George, I'm more interested in getting Ian, that son of a bitch."

"I see. I mean, it can be done, just say the word. I can even help you, if you want?"

"Yeah, I'm going to need your sick brain. And your toys."

With that, Evelyn bided her time, waiting for Ian to think that all had been for-gotten. They still weren't sleeping together, but she pretended that all the tension and anger was gone. Slowly but surely, Ian relaxed, and Evelyn decided that this was the perfect time to act. She started planting her seeds on a Thursday afternoon; she'd had the day off and prepared an elaborate lunch, but not before placing a few short calls. By the time Ian arrived, she was laying on the couch, pretending to have fallen asleep. She heard him enter the kitchen, move around a bit, then come back over to her, gently shaking her shoulder.

"Eve... wake up."

"Hm. What?" She sat up, running a hand through her loose hair. "Go eat, Ruby's coming over later on. Actually, she should be just about on her way." Waiting for him to shuffle back into the kitchen, she checked behind the potted plants for the next step of her plan. *Check*, she thought jubilantly.

For an entire week straight, she went back to being the loving, devoted wife that she had been for years, and Ian was eating it up. It was as if the madness of the past six weeks had never happened, and their lives returned to their regular routine... including church. As much as it killed her to sit in the same room as her husband's gay lover, Evelyn kept it mind that it was all for a very specific purpose, so she sat and even participated, singing the hymns and lining up to take communion. When she reached the front of the line, her eyes met Pastor George's, and she felt a deep sensation of satisfaction to see the pure and abject terror in his eyes before placing the wafer in her mouth. *Yep, this is worth it,* she thought as she sipped the wine and went back to her seat.

Though she knew that the time was ripe to act, she also knew that revenge was a dish best served cold. For that reason, she waited an extra two days to get the ball rolling, secure in the knowledge that she couldn't possibly fail. Turning the television on for some background noise, Evelyn kept checking her watch every few minutes obsessively until she heard a knock at the door.

"That has to be Ruby!" She yelled upstairs. "I'll get it!" Ushering her friend in, they sat around chatting casually when Ruby, projecting her voice, interrupted herself.

"Oh, and here, this is for you, but *don't open it yet*," she insisted with a wink. "I was going to stay but I have Randy boy coming by later, so I've got to run. Ciao."

Knowing perfectly well how nosy her husband was, Evelyn knew that it would only be a matter of time before he would go snooping around. Each time she passed her plants, she checked for any sign of disturbance, but came up empty handed. That is, until one Sunday evening. They continued to go to church, albeit grudgingly on her part. Evelyn quickly tired of going the extra mile in public, so they simply showed their faces and left as soon as service was over. At home, she began to make herself scarce, preferring the solitude of her own thoughts. On one such occasion, she was upstairs in her bedroom reading when suddenly she heard a loud snap and a pained yelp coming from the living room. *Gotcha!* She thought gleefully, finally glad that she'd waited it out.

"Are you all right?" She yelled from the landing. "What did you do?"

"Nothing! I think I stepped on a mouse trap in here. I'm fine," came Ian's upset, strangled voice. *Mouse trap, my* ass, she thought with bitter pleasure. Listening to him struggle in his distress, she hid her smile before going downstairs. Standing at the bottom of the staircase, she stared silently as he frantically tried to remove the contraption from his hand: a harmless looking open mouthed shark plush toy with a spring loaded trap in its mouth.

"Didn't anyone ever tell you to not put your hand where it doesn't belong?" She jeered. Whipping around, his face was pallid with fright.

"What the hell is this?!" All Evelyn could do was giggle uncontrollably, and when she finally composed herself, she tried to find the right words.

"I think the best term for it would be 'just desserts,' I'd say. But not here." Crossing the living room in three long strides, she grabbed the bag and Ian's arm firmly. "Let's go."

"Hey. Yeah, he fell for it. I don't know how to get it off him," Evelyn giggled. "That's your job, hon. I'm on my way now. Great." Ending the call as she drove, she turned to Ian. "We're going to have some fun tonight! Don't worry, it's nothing that you're not already used to, so you'll know exactly what to do." Ian sat frozen in the passenger seat, unable to say a word. Pulling up to Ruby's building, she swung the laden bag over her shoulder as they went upstairs.

"Well, well," Ruby greeted them. "Got your hand stuck in the cookie jar, did we?" She teased. "We'll have to fix that, huh?"

Ruby led him to her mini den, Evelyn following close behind. There, she sat him on a small metal chair while Evelyn dumped the contents of the bag onto the floor. Peering over Ruby's shoulder, Ian saw a handful of assorted dildos, cock cages, and even an ominous looking paddle. Gulping visibly, he final deigned to speak.

"What's all this for?"

"You like being somebody's bitch, so we're giving you the chance to really let loose!" Evelyn said cheerfully. Picking up a toy at random, she turned it over and over in her hands, her expression unreadable. "Do you know what this is? It's a prostate massager. Stand up." Ruby helped him to his feet, the ridiculous plush toy trap still on his hand. Turning him around, they stripped him from the waist down and Evelyn gave him a sound spank on his bare ass. Kneeling behind him, she eased the toy into Ian's ass slowly, deliberately, hearing his sharp intake of breath as the prostate massager hit its mark. "Squeeze real tight, baby," she instructed. "You're going to hold that in, and we'll see how long you last. You don't want to know what we'll do to you if you fail," she warned.

"Check it out, he likes this shit!" Ruby squealed excitedly, pointing at his erection, now standing at half mast.

"You know what to do, then." Skipping away merrily, she produced a cock ring.

"Here we go!" Slipping the ring onto him, he winced at the pressure, opening his mouth to protest. "It's either this or the cage, love. Take your pick." Ian closed his mouth again, involuntarily clenching and making his cock bounce slightly.

"You're not squeezing, babe," Evelyn chided. Leaning in close so that her lips brushed his earlobe, she whispered, "Imagine Pastor George giving you a private tour after service… after he gets done preaching about God and sin. He has, hasn't he? You don't need to tell me. What do they call it again? Carnal sin, is it?"

He nodded emphatically, and a small drop of precum beaded at the tip of his now fully erect cock. "It's carnal sin when you take his meat in your mouth and swallow his cum… or when you fuck his tight asshole with your tongue. It is still tight, isn't it? Or did you take care of that for him?" She reached over and wiggled the prostate massager, making him moan loudly. "That's the answer I like to hear. He's all yours, Ruby." Rubbing her hands together wickedly, Ruby pulled two clothespins out of her back pocket, to everyone's bewilderment. Motioning for him to take off his shirt, she played with the clothespins as she spoke, rubbing them against his bare flesh teasingly.

"Do you like getting your nipples sucked? Most guys I know do," she said conversationally as she clamped Ian. "I'm not too into doing he sucking, myself, but this is a cool alternative, don't you think?"

"Ah, fuck," he growled as Ruby flicked one clothespin. The prostate massager, still lodged in his ass, began to slip, which didn't escape Evelyn's notice.

"I *told* you to keep that thing in!" She picked up the paddle and swung it hard. "Gosh, how hard is it to follow instructions?" Paddling him twice more for good measure, she placed her hands on her hips in a show of frustration. "*What* are we going to do with you?"

Ruby, who was enjoying their game immeasurably, piped up. As full of ideas as she was, she always wanted to try different things, especially if it involved getting her best friend to shed her shyness.

"Ooh! I have something that would hold that in for you," she sang with a malicious glint in her eye. Lifting her dress, she shimmied her underwear off, a pair of lacy blue boyshorts. "See if this helps." With a face burning with shame, Ian put on the boyshorts to the whoops and catcalls of his wife and her best friend. All in all, Ruby was right; the toy did stay in, and his cock was pressed tight against his stomach, the head peeking over the elastic waistband. "My masterpiece," she crooned lovingly.

"Not quite," Evelyn fussed. "Your 'masterpiece' is missing a certain... *je ne sais quoi*." Circling him once, deep in concentration, she snapped her fingers. "I know. Ruby, give me your bra." Ruby pulled down the straps of her dress, expertly undoing her matching bra and taking it off under her clothes. "It would look a whole lot better if you did *this*," Evelyn yanked off the makeshift nipple clamps and fastened the still warm bra behind Ian's back, reaching around to adjust the empty cups. "Now *this* is a masterpiece," she declared proudly.

"H – how do I look?" he asked warily. "Is this what you wanted?"

And there he stood, a man who was once a known and respected head of family, dressed in another woman's bra and underwear while his wife laughed at him. The prostate massager, still lodged deep inside him, kept him from getting soft, but if he were to be totally honest with himself, the humiliation excited him as well.

"Now you look exactly like the faggot bitch that you are!" Evelyn affirmed. "I still have one question for you, though."

"Wh – what?" Ian asked in an unsteady voice. "What's your question?"

Clasping her hands together in front of her, she cocked her head to one side and asked in a sugary sweet tone,

"Do you usually like to fuck or get fucked?" Speechless, Ian open and closed his mouth a few times, unsure of what to say.

"It... depends?" He concluded lamely. "I like getting fucked more," he confessed.

"Ding, ding, ding!" She jeered. "Then today is your lucky day, sweetie pie."

Both women bent him over, forcing him down on all fours, his ass sticking up into the air. Ruby tugged the prostate massager out of him, a loud pop resounding in the room, while Evelyn busied herself with his cock. She pulled the front of his underwear down and it tumbled out, cock ring and all. Gently stroking the underside of his erection with her freshly manicured nails, she saw even more precum leak, and snickered.

"Aww, does somebody want to cum?" she asked in a baby voice. "Will this make you cum? Hm?" He shook his head, making her snort with derision. "Too bad. I guess you won't cum today, after all. I lied." Straightening back up, she gave him a hard shove with her foot, making Ian roll over pathetically. "Now get the hell out of my sight."

An hour later, after having thrown Ian out of the apartment unceremoniously, the two friends sat on her living room floor with yet another bottle of wine.

"So? What now?" Ruby asked, anticipating another wild adventure, now that Evelyn had officially come out of her shell.

"I'm curious to know where you're thinking of going from here."

"No fucking where," she replied flatly, draining her glass and pouring another. "This was fun and all, but I really want to get rid of Ian. Fuck him. You know I whipped the pastor with a bible the other day?" Ruby froze with her own glass halfway to her mouth.

"You did *what*?"

"You heard me. What was I supposed to do? It's all way too much to process right now." Ruby put a comforting arm around her as they fell silent for a short while.

"We could always pay him another visit."